little Miss Quick

by Roger Hargreaves

WORLD INTERNATIONAL
MANCHESTER

Little Miss Quick was always in a terrible hurry and she was always trying to get everything done as quickly as she could.

Now, all this rushing around meant that Little Miss Quick was very careless.

She made her bed so quickly that it was in
more of a mess afterwards than when
she started!

When she brushed her teeth she squeezed
the toothpaste out of the tube so quickly
that it went everywhere.

Everywhere, that is, except on her toothbrush.

One sunny autumn morning,
Little Miss Quick got up even more quickly
than usual, and made her bed and combed
her hair in her quick and careless way.

After a breakfast of bread
(Little Miss Quick was always in far too
much of a hurry to wait for the toaster!)
she ran out of the house like a whirlwind,
and left the door open, as usual.

One minute later,
and three miles from her house,
Little Miss Quick came to a sudden stop.

The postman was standing in her way.

"You have far too many letters to deliver," she said.

"Let me help you."

And she delivered the letters very quickly.

But also very carelessly!

The postman was very angry.

In fact, he was so angry that he chased after Little Miss Quick ...

... but she was already miles away.

She had met Mr Strong.

"That basket of eggs looks very heavy," she said.

"Let me help you carry it back to your house."

And, before Mr Strong had had a chance to say
'no', or even blink for that matter,
Little Miss Quick had carried the eggs back to
his house very quickly ...

... and, needless to say, very carelessly!

When he saw that all his eggs were broken,
Mr Strong was furious.

In fact, he was so furious that he also
chased after Little Miss Quick.

But she was already miles away.

She was at the zoo
talking to the zoo keeper.

"You must be tired of
feeding all these lions,
let me feed them for you," she said.

Then, before you could say 'Little Miss Quick',
she had picked up a bucket of corn and rushed off.

And fed the lions in her usual
quick ... and very careless way.

Lions hate corn!

But they love doors
that are left open.

So it happened that,
on that sunny autumn morning,
Little Miss Quick found herself surrounded
by a very angry postman,
a furious Mr Strong,
a terrified zoo keeper,
and two hungry lions.

What do you think she did?

That's right!

Quick as a shot she said to herself,
"I'd better get out of here as quickly as
ever I can and ...